SEVEN FABLES, SEVEN TRUTHS

Adapted by Dennis Fertig
Illustrated by Carlotta A. Tormey

STECK-VAUGHN
A Harcourt Company

www.steck-vaughn.com

CONTENTS

THE ANTS AND THE GRASSHOPPER

Hard work is important.

It was a fine, crisp winter day. Fresh snow draped field and forest with a clean, white beauty. Beast and bug were happily snuggled away in the warmth of their homes. Each was enjoying the long rest that the cold months bring to those who live in nature.

Well, most were snuggled away. The exception was tall, thin Grasshopper. A lonely creature, he was anything but warm and rested. What little warmth the poor fellow had came from an old scrap of scarf wrapped around his neck. What little rest he took came only from the stops he made now and then as he struggled through the deep snow. But neither warmth nor rest was Grasshopper's first worry. Food was. Grasshopper was hungry—terribly hungry. His hunger was so great that he could not see the beauty of the day.

Under the snow lay the fallen brown leaves, forgotten acorns, and the dried grasses of autumn.

It was not the stuff of a fine meal, but it was food. Grasshopper would gladly have eaten it if he could have reached it. But the wonderful whiteness that covered the ground was too deep. Thick layers of snow made digging for food impossible.

Grasshopper had tried. Only an hour before, he had used his fiddle to dig through the snow. However, a fiddle is not a shovel. Pieces of wood that used to be the fiddle now littered the snow behind him. The instrument of Grasshopper's summer joy would sing no more. Saddened by his loss, Grasshopper pushed on. His long legs pumped slowly in and out of the snow.

After walking a bit longer and finding not a bit of food, Grasshopper fell. He lay on his back and shivered deeply in the cold. When Grasshopper looked up, he saw the empty branches of a huge oak tree above him. Grasshopper struggled to his feet. "I know this tree," he said to himself. "The Ants live near this oak."

Indeed, Grasshopper was right. Deep below the snow where he lay, the Ants were happily passing the afternoon. In the lowest, warmest rooms of their anthill, some napped. Some read. Others played music and danced.

5

THE FATHER AND HIS CHILDREN

United we stand; divided we fall.

It had been a long, bitter Sunday. The weekly family gathering was anything but peaceful. Brothers and sisters argued all afternoon. Father, who loved each of his children equally, worried about how to make peace among them. The arguments that filled the family home every Sunday troubled him deeply. Today stormy weather made things even worse. Gray skies and strong winds added to the unease and unhappiness in the house.

Father knew that the children had not always argued. The disagreements had begun slowly after their mother died. Each of the children missed—and needed—their mother's wise, gentle ways. Those ways had kept peace among the children. In the years since Mother had gone, the children had grown in age. Some were even adults. But their arguing made them seem more and more childish.

Father had tried to stop the arguing. He had gone to each child alone and all of the children together. Again and again he had asked them to work together. He constantly reminded the children that they needed to work together to keep the family and their farm strong.

As Father stared out the window at the gloomy sky, he heard loud voices from the dining room again.

"No!" yelled John, his oldest son. "We cannot plant the fields yet. Winter is still here. The seeds will die in the cold."

The children looked at each other and wondered why their Father would bring a bundle of sticks into the house.

"John," Father said. "You are the strongest in the family. No one can argue about that."

"He may have the strongest body," said Martha, "but I have the strongest mind."

Suddenly five voices of the other children yelled as one. "No, I do!"

"Children! Silence!" commanded Father.

When the children hushed, Father continued. "John, pick up the bundle of twigs and try to break it in half."

John looked at his father. "That will be easy, Father. It's just a bundle of twigs."

Father smiled, and John tried. And tried. Then he tried some more. He couldn't break the bundle in half. "I cannot do it, Father," said John. The other children laughed a little.

Father said, "Each of you must try."

They each did. The bundle was passed from to Martha to Michael to Margaret to William and to Louise. Each worked hard to break the bundle, but none could.

Father took the bundle from Louise. He untied the string and gave each of his children a single twig. "Try to break those," he said.

Six snaps echoed in the dining room. Each of the children had easily broken a twig.

Father sighed and said, "My children, if you are of one mind and work to help each other, you will be like the bundle. You will be unbroken by the hardships of life. But if you stay divided among yourselves, you will be broken as easily as each twig. Then our fields and our family will fail. The farm will be lost."

Silence followed for a moment. Then John said, "You are right, Father. United we stand. Divided we fall." The other five children nodded their heads together. At last, all the children were in agreement.

MERCURY AND THE WOODCUTTER

Honesty is rewarded.

Woodcutter was proud of his job. Every day he worked hard in the forest. Some of the trees that he cut down became boards used to build homes, boats, and wagons. Other trees became fuel for cooking and warmth. None of the wood was wasted.

Woodcutter knew the work that he and his fellow workers did was important. Their hard work meant survival for their large families and poor village. In Woodcutter's mind, no job was more important than his. Nothing he owned was more special than his ax. Its sharp blade helped him in his work. Without his ax, he could not support his family or help his village.

At the moment, however, the sound of something much different filled the forest. It was Woodcutter's loud sobs. Crying was not what Woodcutter did best, but it was all he could do just now. The unhappy fellow had lost his ax. While he was chopping a large tree

near a lake, he had let his treasured tool slip from his
grip. The ax flew into the lake, a body of water widely
feared for its cold, dark depths. The happiness of
Woodcutter's family and village lay at the bottom
of the lake.

The more Woodcutter thought about his loss, the
louder his sobs grew. Finally their volume caught the
ear of the mighty Mercury, who was traveling near the
forest. As Woodcutter sat on a log in the forest and
cried loudly into his hands, Mercury approached
quietly. He observed the weeping Woodcutter for a
moment or two.

"Woodcutter, why do you wail so?" Mercury suddenly demanded.

Woodcutter had no idea he had company and was shocked by the powerful voice. He looked up, blinked the tears out of his eyes, and stared at mighty Mercury. Of course, he knew about Mercury. Mercury was a very unusual being. He looked human, but he was bigger, stronger, and more handsome than most humans. More important, Mercury had powers and wisdom well beyond that of a normal man or woman. If he were in the right mood, Mercury might use his special gifts to help humans. If he were in the wrong mood, most creatures, human or otherwise, found it best to avoid him.

"Sir," said Woodcutter nervously, "my grief comes from my foolishness. I am a miserable woodcutter who lost his ax in the depths of this horrible lake."

Mercury eyed Woodcutter and the lake for a moment. He silently agreed that the Woodcutter did indeed look miserable and that the lake looked horrible. Mercury sensed that Woodcutter was a good man. "But," thought Mercury to himself, "of what value are my powers if I cannot use them to test these poor humans?"

With the slightest twinkle in his eye, Mercury said, "Woodcutter, I will help you in your time of trouble. I will find and return your ax."

As soon as he spoke these words, Mercury plunged into the dark lake. Seconds later, he bobbed to the top, holding up a gold ax that glimmered richly in the afternoon sun.

"Woodcutter, is this your ax?" roared Mercury.

"No, sir," said the disappointed Woodcutter. "But thank you for trying."

"The fellow will not claim a gold ax!" said Mercury to himself as he dived beneath the dark water again.

Seconds later, Mercury once again bobbed to the top of the lake. In his powerful fist he held up a silver ax that shone brightly.

"Woodcutter, is this your ax?" roared Mercury.

"No, sir," said the even more disappointed Woodcutter. "But thank you again for trying."

"This fellow will not even claim a silver ax!" said Mercury to himself as he dived into the dark water for a third time.

Once again Mercury bobbed to the top of the water. This time he held up Woodcutter's lost ax. "Woodcutter, is this your ax?" roared Mercury.

"Yes, sir," said the happy man. "Thank you!"

"My good fellow, you have impressed me with your honesty," said Mercury. "In fact, you have so impressed me that I shall give you the gold and silver axes as well."

Woodcutter was grateful for Mercury's generosity. The gold and silver would aid his poor family and village. After his working day was over, Woodcutter joined the other woodcutters on the path back to the village. He told them about his good fortune. He did not notice that one of his listeners quickly disappeared back into the forest.

The listener was a man with a plan. Wanting the same good fortune as Woodcutter, he ran to the lake and threw his own ax into the murky water. The man then sat down on the bank and began to cry loudly. Mercury heard the man's wails and quietly came to learn who was making them.

"Sir," said the foolish man when he saw Mercury before him. "I lost my ax in the lake. Will you help me find it?"

Mercury had doubts about this fellow but decided to treat him as he had the first man.

"I shall return your ax, friend," said Mercury. As before, he plunged into the lake.

In only seconds Mercury swam to the top of the lake. He was holding up a gold ax. "Friend, is this your ax?" he asked the foolish man.

Greed flashed in the man's eyes. He grabbed the ax and said, "Yes, that is the ax I lost!"

Mercury rose completely from the lake and angrily stared down at the man. "Dishonest man, this is not your ax," Mercury said quietly. He then ripped the gold ax from the fellow's hand and threw it back into the water. "Your ax is still at the bottom of the lake, where it will stay. Perhaps your loss will teach you that honesty is the best policy." Mercury smiled and was gone.

The dishonest man turned and walked back to the village, where his sad cries were heard long before he arrived.

THE HORSE AND THE MULE

Selfishness can bring unhappiness.

Old Woman, Horse, and Mule walked slowly up a trail. The three carried crops from the farms on one side of a mountain to the village on the other side. On the return trip, they carried tools, flour, and other supplies from the village back to the farms.

The only path between the village and the farms went over the mountain. Much of the trail was steep, so the journey was always a hard one. Old Woman and Mule had been making it for many years. When they were younger, trips over the mountain had seemed fast. Now both were always tired. The distance between the farms and village seemed longer and longer.

Horse had joined them a few years before. She was young and strong. She was sometimes so full of energy that she trotted ahead of the other two. For Horse, the journey was boring. She filled it with dreams of apples in the village and oats at the farms.

This day was the hottest of the summer. But hot or
not, the three were on their usual journey to the village.
Both Horse and Mule carried heavy loads. Even Old
Woman carried a heavy pack on her back. All would
have preferred resting in the cool shade, but each had
to work to eat. As always, they marched on.

Although she was hot, Horse had no particular
trouble with her load. Carrying it was hard enough,
and she would rather not do it at all, but she had
carried heavier loads on other hot days.

For Mule, it wasn't so simple. As long as the three traveled along the flat parts of the trail, he could handle the load. Large, leafy trees shaded the flat parts. The steep parts of the mountain trail were different. They had no trees, so the hot sun beat down on them.

When the three began to climb the rocky mountain path on this day, Mule's load felt heavier than any he could remember. For the first time in his long years as a beast of burden, Mule wondered if he was carrying too much. "Friend Horse," said Mule after the three had climbed a short way up the trail. "This weight suddenly feels like more than I can bear. Is it possible that you might carry a bit of it for me? I am sure that if you take a little, I can carry the rest to the village."

Horse was surprised. In the years she had traveled with these two companions, she had never heard a word of complaint from Mule or Old Woman. In fact, the only complaining she had ever heard on the trail was her own.

Even though she was surprised, Horse did not care about Mule's problem. "Of course I cannot help you," answered Horse. "You must carry your own load, just as I must carry mine."

Mule walked on in silence and pain. Old Woman could not understand the language of four-legged animals. Still, she was smart and knew Mule well from their years together. Old Woman guessed that the load was too great for her longtime partner.

"Old friend, I think your load is a bit heavy," said Old Woman. "I will carry some of it myself." Old Woman then took a bag of potatoes from Mule's load and put it under her arm.

Horse watched with fear and then amusement. The fear was that Old Woman might make her carry the potatoes. When that did not happen, Horse was amused by the Old Woman's decision. "Only a stupid creature would choose a heavier burden," Horse thought to herself.

If Old Woman knew Horse's thoughts, she did not show it. She was just glad that Mule's load was a little lighter.

Old Woman's kind act did help Mule for a while. Soon, though, Mule was once more struggling against the heat and difficult climb. The three had climbed a little farther when Mule's load again felt heavier than any he had ever carried.

Mule hid his pain from Old Woman but spoke again to Horse. "Young friend, I may soon collapse under this load. I beg you to take a bit of it to help me," he said.

Horse shook her head. "If you cannot carry your own weight, have Old Woman carry it," she said. "I will not increase my load for you."

Mule was disappointed but tried not to show it. He was afraid Old Woman would take more of the burden and do herself harm. But Old Woman was observant. She saw pain in Mule's face and a slight stumble in Mule's walk. "Old friend," she said to Mule, "we will—" Before Old Woman could say "rest," Mule brayed loudly and fell down on the path.

Old Woman rushed to Mule's side. "Ah, you are still breathing, old friend," she said to Mule. "We must get you to the village."

Old Woman ordered Horse to kneel. She then took the load off Mule's back. With great effort she pushed and pulled Mule onto Horse's back. Then Old Woman took Mule's load and put that on Horse's back, too. Finally, the tired Old Woman put the sack of potatoes she had been carrying on Horse's back as well. Old Woman then pulled Horse to a standing position.

Horse groaned beneath the new load. She took a few slow steps. Old Woman said to her, "Young friend, your load is heavy, but you are strong. We must hurry to the village and get help for Mule."

Horse's back ached, and she realized what her selfishness had cost her. She looked over her shoulder at Mule. "I deserve this," she said to him. "I should have helped you a little. If I had, I would not have to carry you, your burden, and my burden as well. My selfishness has brought me unhappiness."

Old Woman then led the slow-moving Horse over the rugged mountain trail.

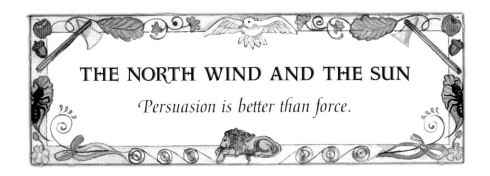

THE NORTH WIND AND THE SUN

Persuasion is better than force.

A lone man in a red cloak walked across a fine field of deep green grass and bright blue flowers. Sun shone warmly down on him. North Wind blew softly, gently rustling the man's cloak. The man whistled quietly to himself. He thought only about the beauty of the day. Because he was only a human, the poor fellow had no idea of the great argument going on high above him. He could not know that the distant skies echoed with the angry words that two powerful forces threw at each other.

"I am more powerful than you, Sun!" roared North Wind. "I will prove it!"

Sun smiled warmly, in spite of his anger. "North Wind, you do not know my power. Set a test for us, and I will show it to you."

North Wind looked down at the earth. He saw the fine field of deep green grass and bright blue flowers.

Then North Wind noticed the man walking along all by himself. He listened to the man's happy whistling. "I will show you my power!" yelled North Wind to Sun. "I shall force the red cloak off that man's back."

Suddenly North Wind blew with all his might, aiming at the man's cloak. The lone walker had not heard North Wind's bragging, but he felt North Wind's blast. The force of North Wind's power nearly knocked him down. The man stopped his whistling. He pulled his cloak tighter around himself, hunched over a bit, and then walked on.

North Wind blew again and again. The man pulled his cloak tighter and kept walking as best as he could. The stronger the blast, the tighter the man wrapped his cloak around himself.

After blowing over and over, North Wind realized he would not succeed. He could not blow the red cloak off the man, so as suddenly as the cold blasts came, they stopped. The day returned to its earlier charm. The man walked straight and tall, loosened the grip on his cloak, and started to whistle again.

"I have failed, but can you succeed?" North Wind asked Sun.

"I will, my friend," said Sun. The walker could not hear Sun's words, but he felt their effect. Sun suddenly shone out with all its warmth.

The walker no sooner felt Sun's golden rays than he said to himself, "Ah, the sweetness of the day has returned." He took off his red cloak and smiled up toward the sky. As he walked along, he thought about what had happened. "It was as if the wind tried to blow my cloak off and failed," he thought. "Then the sun gently warmed me, and I took my cloak off on my own. I must remember the lesson I have learned today—persuasion is better than force."

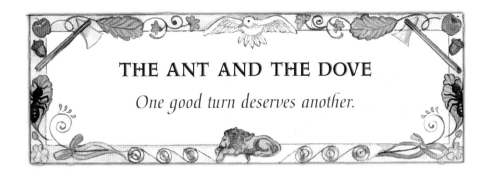

THE ANT AND THE DOVE

One good turn deserves another.

Ant heard the rushing stream before he saw it. It was a pleasing sound, for Ant was thirsty. He climbed over several pebbles—a long distance for such a tiny creature—and viewed the rippling stream. It flowed swiftly and could be dangerous for a creature as small as he. Yet Ant wasn't afraid because he did not plan on going into the stream. He just wanted a drink.

Ant moved closer to the stream. Then he carefully perched himself on its muddy edge and took a sip of the cold, clean water. As Ant drank, his front legs slowly started to slip toward the stream. At first Ant did not notice. But when his second set of legs slipped, Ant knew he was in trouble. He was about to fall into the water. Ant frantically tried to dig his third set of legs into the muddy edge, but the small insect's efforts were useless. He fell headfirst into the fast flow of the stream.

Perhaps Ant's brothers and sisters would have been strong enough to save themselves if they fell in. Ant was not. The rushing stream spun him around and around. In seconds it would force him under the water forever.

Next to the stream stood an old oak tree. One of its branches reached out over the water where Ant struggled to stay alive. On the branch sat Dove, who was resting and enjoying the sound of the bubbling stream below her. Dove saw Ant at the very moment he fell into the water. Her quick mind saw Ant's dangerous problem. Her kind heart found a solution.

Dove tore a leaf from the oak tree and let it fall into the stream below. It landed on the water right in front of Ant. Ant saw the leaf and reached for it but missed. He reached a second time and missed. Ant reached a third time and caught just the edge of the leaf. It was enough. Ant pulled himself onto the leaf and floated safely to the edge of the stream.

When he was on land, Ant scrambled up the muddy bank to dry grass. As he lay in the grass, breathing hard, he looked upward at Dove. Ant realized Dove had saved him and said weakly, "Thank you for your kindness, Dove."

"It was nothing," said Dove and flew away.

Dove was not only kind but beautiful. She was so beautiful that many humans would have kept her in a cage in their home. Although Dove's beauty would have made a human's house more pleasant, Dove did not wish to live in a cage.

One human hiding in the woods that morning did not care about Dove's wish to be free. His name was Bird Catcher.

Bird Catcher caught and sold beautiful birds to other humans. He had often seen Dove in the big oak tree. He knew he could sell her for a high price, so he made a trap of twigs and string. In the center of the trap he placed some seeds that Dove would like. Bird Catcher's plan was simple. When Dove flew down to eat the seeds, he would pull the string and make the trap fall over Dove. All Bird Catcher had to do was hide and wait in the tall grass.

After Ant had caught his breath, he wandered off to continue his work for the day. He had climbed back over the pebbles when he saw something moving in the tall grass. It was Bird Catcher. Ant was standing right next to Bird Catcher's big feet.

Ant did not know who Bird Catcher was or what he did for living, but Ant did see the string in Bird Catcher's hand. Ant also saw that the string led to the trap that held the seeds. Then Ant noticed Dove in the sky above, and Bird Catcher's plan became clear. When Dove started to fly down toward the seeds, Ant leaped at Bird Catcher and stung him on the ankle. Bird Catcher jumped up quickly, howled in pain, and ran away. His noise frightened Dove, who flew away.

After a moment Dove circled back to see what had happened. She saw the trap and the string. She also saw Ant lying on the ground where Bird Catcher had been. As Ant stood up, Dove swooped over him and said, "Thank you!"

Ant smiled up at her. "It was nothing," he said. "After all, one good turn deserves another."

THE TWO HUNTERS

Heroes are brave in actions as well as words.

Two hunters, one large and one small, set out hunting together. Their goal was to find the tracks of the lion, the mightiest beast of the land. The hunters were well prepared for their trip. They carried food and water. They even carried drawings to help them recognize the prints of the Lion's paws.

Big Hunter said, "I am ready to find the tracks of the Lion. I am ready to walk where the Lion has gone before."

Little Hunter agreed. "I am ready to find the Lion's tracks, too," he said. "I want nothing more than to trace the steps of the mighty beast."

"We are very brave hunters," said Big Hunter. "Surely no hunters have ever been so brave."

As the hunters walked through the forest, they met other people doing important things, but nothing as important as their search.

They met Bird Catcher on a little hill near a stream. "I search for beautiful birds," Bird Catcher said to the two hunters.

"Your hunt requires skill, but ours requires bravery," said Big Hunter. "We go to find the tracks of the Lion. We are ready to put our hands and feet in the giant pawprints that the Lion has left."

"I agree with my friend, noble Bird Catcher. Your hunt is interesting," said Little Hunter. "But we seek the tracks of the king of beasts. We are eager to walk where the mighty Lion has gone."

"It is an honor meet you," said Bird Catcher to the hunters.

Big Hunter and Little Hunter went on their way. One morning they crossed a green field filled with bright blue flowers. There they met a man in a red cloak. "Friend, what is your goal as you walk through this field?" Big Hunter asked the walker.

"My goal is a simple one," answered the walker. "I wish to enjoy the beauty of the day. I wish to feel the warm sunshine upon my face."

"You are a good man—a poet, no doubt," said Little Hunter. "However, our goal is better than yours. We are looking for the tracks of the Lion. We are eager to march in the path of the most powerful animal on the earth."

"Perhaps you will write a poem about our journey," said Big Hunter. "Then everyone will know how brave we are. They will know how far we have traveled to find the trail left by the king of beasts."

The lone walker smiled. "It has been an honor to meet you," he said.

As the two hunters hiked on, they neared a dark, deep lake in a forest. At the lake's edge, they met Woodcutter. He was swinging his ax into a large tree.

"Powerful Woodcutter, you work with such energy!" said Big Hunter.

"Yes, my hard work feeds my family and helps my village," he replied.

"Hard work is good," said Little Hunter. "But we are heroes. We seek the trail of the Lion. Everyone will know that we are brave when we place our feet in his tracks."

"Tell your family and village that we are looking for the tracks of the Lion," added Big Hunter. "We wish to find the path that it has taken."

Woodcutter looked at Big Hunter and Little Hunter. "My friends, you are very lucky today!" he said.

The two hunters smiled.

"I know where the Lion is," said Woodcutter. "I can lead you right to him. He lives nearby."

The two hunters lost their smiles and turned very pale. Big Hunter, his teeth chattering with fear, said, "No, thank you. We did not ask to find the Lion."

"No, indeed," agreed Little Hunter with tears of fright in his eyes. "It is only his tracks we search for, not the Lion himself."

Woodcutter saw the two hunters' fear but wasn't surprised. He said to them, "You are not brave. Heroes are brave in actions as well as their words."

The speechless hunters turned and fled the forest, leaving nets and supplies behind them. Before Woodcutter began to swing his ax again, he smiled a smile no one else saw.